PUFFIN BOOKS
The Bangers and Chips Explosion

Billy Baxter and his school friends are going on strike. They are fed up with eating salads every day for school dinners. When the Head advertises for some new cooks they are optimistic, and can't believe their luck when suddenly their favourite food, chips, are on the menu every day!

Unfortunately, the cooks aren't really interested in frying chips. They are none other than Hairy Harry the Hatchet Man and his horrible gang of crooks. A nasty mistake brought them to St Gertrude's Junior School, but once there they are determined to make it a rewarding experience. Suddenly the Head disappears . . .

No one knows what to do until the cool and confident school secretary, Mrs Perkins, comes up with a plan of action. But the crooks stop at nothing and nothing, it seems, can save Billy and his friends. Mrs Perkins is out on her own and faces the greatest challenge of her life. When all appears lost, she pulls out a few surprises!

This is a very funny, action-packed adventure story full of some delightful (and some horrible) characters.

When Brough Girling was a boy, his favourite food was sausage, egg and chips. It still is.

D1324809

Brough Girling

The Bangers and Chips Explosion

Illustrated by Tony Blundell

PUFFIN BOOKS

PUFFIN BOOKS

Published by the Penguin Group
27 Wrights Lane, London W8 5TZ, England
Viking Penguin Inc., 40 West 23rd Street, New York, New York 10010, USA
Penguin Books Australia Ltd, Ringwood, Victoria, Australia
Penguin Books Canada Ltd, 2801 John Street, Markham, Ontario, Canada L3R 1B4
Penguin Books (NZ) Ltd, 182–190 Wairau Road, Auckland 10, New Zealand

Penguin Books Ltd, Registered Offices: Harmondsworth, Middlesex, England

First published 1989
5 7 9 10 8 6 4

Copyright © Brough Girling, 1989
Illustrations copyright © Tony Blundell, 1989
All rights reserved

Made and printed in Great Britain by
Cox & Wyman, Reading
Typeset in Linotron 202 Century Schoolbook
Centracet, Cambridge

This book is dedicated with
respect and trepidation
to school secretaries, everywhere.

Chapter One

*

'Please, Sir . . .' said Billy Baxter, knocking on the office door.

'What is it, Billy?' said Mr Mackintosh, the Head Teacher.

'Please, Sir – we're going on strike.'

'Now, don't be so ridiculous, Billy!' said the Head Teacher with a frown. 'Whatever do you think you are talking about?'

'I'm talking about going on strike. We're going on strike because there are no chips!'

'NO CHIPS!' said Mr Mackintosh. He got up from behind his desk. 'Now look here, Billy Baxter, I have heard some nonsense in my time, but I have never in all my born days come across anything as idiotic as schoolchildren going on strike over no chips! I think you had better sit down and tell me all about it.'

It's not much fun being a Head Teacher at the best of times, he thought to himself, but today is definitely *not* my lucky day.

'Well, Mr Mackintosh, there were no chips yesterday, or the day before that, or the day before that, and then it was last weekend, but all last week we didn't have chips once. It's salad today, and it was salad yesterday, and the day before . . .'

'All right!' interrupted Mr Mackintosh. 'You needn't go on about it. I take it that you like chips?'

'Like them . . . we adore them. We love them. We're all chipoholics! Chipetarians! Chips are bread and butter to us.'

The Head Teacher was suddenly aware of chanting coming from the playground. It started softly, but then the sound grew.

'*We want chips! We want chips! WE WANT CHIPS!*'

'*What do we want?*'

'*CHIPS!*'

'*What do we want?*'

'*CHIPS! CHIPS! CHIPS!*'

'This is terrible,' said the Head with a groan. 'I have

enough trouble if *teachers* go on strike – let alone children. I'll be the laughing-stock of the whole county.'

His heart sank at the thought of it. What on earth was he going to do? Perhaps he had better call the school secretary into the office – maybe she could help him talk some sense into the silly boy.

Mrs Janet Perkins sat at a small desk in a room that joined Mr Mackintosh's office. With a weary sigh, he asked her to come in and he explained his terrible problem to her.

'Well, Billy,' she said in a voice that was firm but kind. 'If you call off your action now, I'll go and have a word with Mrs Gunge in the kitchen on your behalf, and see what she says. I think that going on strike over chips is a very silly and naughty thing to do, but I'm prepared to be reasonable by offering to help you in this way. Now off you go back to the playground.'

'Yes, Mrs Perkins,' said Billy Baxter, and he left the room.

'Don't worry, Head Master, I'll try to sort this one out,' said Mrs Perkins, and off she went to see Mrs Gunge.

Mrs Gunge was the Chief Cook and Dinner Lady at St Gertrude's Junior School.

Have you ever noticed that there are only two types of dinner lady? They are either very nice or very nasty. Mrs Gunge was very nasty. She looked damp and greasy. She had thick, knobbly, cabbage-stalk legs and her chin had lumps on it with white whiskers coming out of them. If you found a hair in your salad at St Gertrude's, you gave your plate to someone else.

Mrs Perkins thoroughly disliked Mrs Gunge, not just because she was repulsive, but because she was lazy and slapdash and wasn't nice to the children.

9

When Mrs Perkins got to the school kitchens, she found Mrs Gunge in the middle of peeling a sackful of carrots. 'Ah, Mrs Gunge,' she said, 'I need a word with you. The Head Teacher is having a bit of trouble with the children . . .'

'Kids!' said Mrs Gunge with a snarl. 'There's only one thing wrong with this rotten school . . . *it's got kids in it*! Why doesn't someone invent a school full of just dinner ladies – then we'd have a lot less trouble.'

She blew out through her toothless mouth in disgust. It was like the lips of some deep-sea fish sifting salt water for plankton.

'It seems . . .' Mrs Perkins went on in a firm tone, 'that they would like a lot less salad, and a lot more chips.'

'Well, they can't have it! Why should kids always get what they want? Spoilt little brats! From now on it's going to be lettuce and raw carrot and yoghurt for afters. So there!'

'Couldn't they have chips with their salads, say once a week?' asked Mrs Perkins, trying to be reasonable.

'NO!' said Mrs Gunge. She put her red hands firmly on her hips, and glared.

'Well, if that's your attitude, I'm afraid I'll have to recommend to the Head that he calls in a catering firm. He and I can't cope with pupils going on strike – it's bad enough when they're working.'

'I shouldn't call in a catering firm if I was you,' hissed Mrs Gunge. 'We had one here before you came. They didn't last a week. The gravy was so thick you had to carve it! Even the staff-room tea had lumps in it. In fact, it was the staff going on strike that time that finally got rid of them. I came instead.'

'Well, there is another solution . . .' said Mrs Perkins, turning on her heels and leaving the room in a swirl of cardigan.

Mrs Gunge sniffed, blew her nose on a damp lettuce leaf, and got on with the salads.

Mrs Perkins went back to the Head Teacher's office.

'I'm sorry, Mr Mackintosh,' she said. 'Mrs Gunge seems quite determined not to co-operate, and so if we're not careful we'll have an all-out strike to deal with. On the other hand, I think it's a first-class opportunity to employ some better cooks, and to show Mrs Gunge that *you* run this school, not her. She doesn't care a jot for the children. She needs bringing down a peg or two. I think the best thing would be to put an advert in tonight's newspaper advertising for some new school cooks. Then, with a bit of luck, you will be able to replace her.'

'You are quite right, of course,' said the Head. 'I'll do it this instant. It's the only way to get out of this terrible situation.'

He closed his eyes and started to compose an advertisement which, although he did not know it at the time, was to open a new and dramatic page in the history of St Gertrude's Junior School.

COOKS WANTED

TO WORK IN A CHALLENGING BUT
REWARDING ENVIRONMENT
MUST BE CO-OPERATIVE AND
HAVE IMAGINATION

APPLY TO:
THE HEAD
ST GERTRUDE'S JUNIOR SCHOOL

Chapter Two

In which we meet two more very nasty pieces of work,
and learn that not all newspapers can spell.

*

The next day, in another part of the town, in a hide-
out that would have made Fungus the Bogeyman's
lavatory look like the inside of a dry cleaner's, one of
the world's worst criminals was feeling rather sorry
for himself.

His name was Hairy Harry, but his friends called
him Hairy Harry the Hatchet Man. He was built like
a mountain. He was bigger than a gorilla, bigger than
a Russian hammer-thrower – man or woman, bigger
and fiercer than any school dinner lady. He didn't just
have cauliflower ears – he had a cauliflower nose, a
cauliflower face and a cauliflower head.

He was feeling sorry for himself because he was
bored. He had only recently come out of prison, and
he hadn't found anything interesting or criminal to
do.

'If only . . .' he said aloud to himself. 'If only all the
rest of the lads in my gang were here, we could get
together and do something interesting, like having a
go at the crown jewels. If only . . .'

He twiddled his great hairy thumbs. Harry the
Hatchet Man was *very* hairy. He didn't just have hair
on the back of his hands, he had it on the front of them,
too, *and* behind his knees, *and* between his toes, *and*

on the soles of his feet. He looked like a hearthrug that needed to be thrown away.

But I must warn you that Harry wasn't just repulsive to look at – he also had a repellent personality. He was the most frightful man you could wish not to meet. You wouldn't want to meet him at a tea party, let alone in a dark alleyway at night when the moon's gone behind a cloud. He always carried an axe under his coat. AAHHH! STAY INDOORS IF HAIRY HARRY THE HATCHET MAN IS HAVING A NIGHT OUT!

So Harry sat there in his revolting den, looking miserable. It was deep in a cellar beneath the ruins of some derelict houses below some waste land. The walls dripped with green slime and the spluttering candles gave off thick greasy black smoke. The place was not fit for rat habitation; Harry felt quite at home there.

Suddenly there was a knock at the door. Harry reached for his axe and went to answer it. 'Who's there?' he demanded.

'Me,' said a voice from the alleyway outside.

'Who's me?' said Harry, raising his axe to shoulder height in case it was the police.

'Me! Sid!' said the voice.

'Sid!' said Hairy Harry, a big beaming smile lighting up his horrible features. He opened the door, and there outside was none other than his old friend and partner in several crimes, Cyanide Sid.

Cyanide Sid was small and fat. His speciality was poisoning people. He did it all the time. He could mix up brews that were far, far worse than any medicine your mother's ever given you. His drinks could rot you from the inside in two seconds flat. In his time he had got steam to come out of people's ears, he had turned them purple and melted their teeth.

15

Yuk!

'Hey, Boss,' said Sid. 'Great to see you again!'

'Great to see you, too, Sid! I was just thinking about you and the other lads. I didn't know if you were still out and about. How are you?'

'To be honest, I'm bored, Boss. I've only just come out of prison and I haven't poisoned anyone for ages and ages. I'm really fed up, I can tell you!'

'That's odd . . .' said Harry slowly – he always spoke rather slowly because it took him a long time to think of the next word – 'I was just feeling exactly the same thing. I haven't done a worthwhile job since *I* came out of the jug either!'

'How about getting together again?' said Sid more cheerfully. 'There must be a bank or fur shop or jeweller round here that we could have a go at. I can poison the owner while you remove the safe and empty the till. Let's have a look in the paper.'

As he said it he took a copy of the evening paper from under his fat little arm, and he and Harry spread it out on the filthy table. Harry turned the pages with his huge banana fingers.

When they got to the adverts, a large one in the middle of the page caught their attention, though some time afterwards they probably wished that it hadn't.

This is what it said:

CROOKS WANTED

TO WORK IN A CHALLENGING BUT
REWARDING ENVIRONMENT
MUST BE CO-OPERATIVE AND
HAVE IMAGINATION

APPLY TO:
THE HEAD
ST GERTRUDE'S JUNIOR SCHOOL

You've guessed it: the newspaper had made a disastrous spelling mistake.

Chapter Three

In which two unsuitable people start a new job.

*

'Here!' said Cyanide Sid. 'What about this then? CROOKS WANTED. That's us, isn't it?'

'WANTED!' said Hairy Harry. 'Of course we're blooming wanted. I've been among the most wanted people in the country ever since I left junior school!'

'Hang on, it may not be that sort of wanted,' replied his horrible little friend. 'I reckon it's some guy with a really beefy job up his sleeve. He probably plans to rob a bank or something like that, and he wants the right kind of people to assist him. "Rewarding" – you know what that means – that there's a good amount of loot in it, specially if we're "co-operative" with him. And "imaginative" just means people who can think fast enough not to get caught.'

'I've been caught quite a few times,' said Hairy Harry, and a large tear began to roll down his cheek as he thought of the many years he'd frittered away in Her Majesty's prisons.

'Well, I don't think anyone with any sense is going to get caught on *this* job,' said Sid. 'This Head fellow is obviously a professional. As we haven't got any money, and we're not having any fun poisoning anyone or anything like that, why don't we give it a try?'

'You're quite right, Sid, quite right,' said Harry. 'We'll go round to see him tomorrow.'

18

The very next day, Hairy Harry and Cyanide Sid drove their getaway van up the drive of St Gertrude's Junior School and went straight in to see Mr Mackintosh. Several days later they wished they hadn't.

'We've come about the job in the paper, Guv,' said Hairy Harry to the rather startled Head Teacher.

'I see,' he said. 'Do you have any experience?'

'EXPERIENCE! I'll say we does,' said Harry with a chuckle. 'We've done years between us, haven't we, Sid?'

Sid agreed that between them they had done years.

'And can you do all the usual recipes?' asked the Head.

'You bet!' said Cyanide Sid. He was short and very fat, and looked as if he'd sampled a lot of good cooking in his time.

'Can you be creative with quite basic ingredients?'

'You bet I can,' said Sid with a sneer. 'I specialize in putting unusual things together and achieving quite spectacular results.' He was thinking of the time he had wiped out a gang in Chicago with a large lemon meringue and paraquat pie.

'Well,' said the Head, 'I must admit I'm pretty desperate.'

'Oh, I'm desperate as well, Guv,' said Hairy Harry, a large grin lighting up his face as he remembered the time a high-court judge had told him that he was 'a desperate criminal and a menace to society'.

'Very well,' said Mr Mackintosh, 'you can start work straight away. Mrs Gunge will show you round the school kitchens.'

And so it was that two of the most unsuitable people in the world started work in the kitchens of one of our quieter and more refined junior schools.

It didn't take Hairy Harry the Hatchet Man very long to get the hang of school life. He enjoyed the next few days, and grew to like several things about work in the kitchens.

He was very fond of cutting up the meat for school stew. He used the biggest knife in the kitchen, two-handed, smashing it down from above his head into lumps of raw steak – like some ghastly executioner.

He nearly made a bad mistake on the second day.
Cyanide Sid told him to look in the school fridge for
some jelly, and Harry thought he meant gelignite. He
couldn't find any gelignite in the fridge so he went out
to the van for some; there was always plenty in the
back in case it should come in handy. Sid stopped him
just in time before he served it out to the infants.

Cyanide Sid was in his element, even though Hairy
Harry had warned him not to poison anyone until they
had found out what job their new employer was really
planning for them.

'Go easy on the arsenic in the first few weeks, Sid,'
Harry had said, and when Harry gave you an instruc-
tion it was usually sensible to follow it.

Sid did his best to make wholesome, unpoisonous food. He really looked the part, with his fat figure tucked up inside his white chef's uniform.

'I hope you two are getting the hang of the job,' said Mr Mackintosh, popping his head round the kitchen door on the morning of their fourth day.

'What job, Guv?' asked Hairy Harry. 'I've been in on a lot of "jobs" in my time – when is this job going to start?'

But the Head Teacher did not hear him. He was walking back towards his office, smiling with pleasure at the way he had dealt so smoothly with Billy Baxter's ridiculous chip strike.

Chapter Four

In which Hairy Harry has a surprisingly bright idea.

*

St Gertrude's Junior School was soon full of smiling children. There were chips with everything, every day. Hairy Harry and Cyanide Sid were fond of chips themselves, and the two of them spent many a jolly morning peeling and slicing. The school kitchen was filled with the sound of their merry whistling and the singing sizzle of the deep-fat frier as another load spluttered its way to crisp brown perfection.

Sid – always fussy about getting recipes just right – knew that a satisfying chip is soft and white on the inside but golden brown on the outside: he tried lots of them to make sure he got them spot on.

There were burgers and chips, egg and chips, just chips, chips with tomato sauce, stew and chips, mince and chips, chips bolognaise, lasagne and chips, chips with extra chips, chips with gravy, with blancmange, chips with custard, jelly and chips, chips with Angel Topping. Sid even tried to make chip soup.

Billy Baxter was specially pleased, and so were the children in his class.

'Hey, Billy,' said Jim Tucket in the playground one day, 'I reckon that strike threat of yours worked. The new cooks Big Mac has got in are really good at chips!'

'Yes,' agreed their friend, Yashpal. 'Mrs Gunge isn't

too pleased, though. She says we should all be eating salad and yoghurts!'

'She's horrible, and she looks *extra* grumpy,' added Belinda Bollard.

What Belinda said was quite true. Mrs Gunge was very far from pleased to have two new cooks in her kitchen, and her enemy Mrs Perkins had told her that she was now simply a dinner lady and no longer Chief Cook.

Mrs Gunge had always hated Mrs Perkins, and she knew that it was she who had persuaded the Head to employ new cooks. She began to burn with resentment, like a witch who decides it's time to nobble someone with a really horrible, liver-scorching spell! She was determined to have her revenge.

As she shovelled out the chips at lunch times, she mumbled things to herself through her whiskery, toothless mouth: 'I'll show that Mrs Perkins ... I'll teach her a lesson ... and just let *him* wait and see. School secretaries and Head Teachers should be put down at birth! No one messes Mrs Gloria Gunge about without regretting it.'

Soon the demand for chips at lunch time grew so great that Harry and Sid had difficulty in making enough of them. Harry tried to speed up the process by attacking the peeled potatoes with his axe, but that was still not fast enough.

Then they would over-react and make too many!

'What we'll have to do, Sid,' Harry said very slowly one morning, 'is go round the classrooms and ask the kids how many chips they think they are going to eat. Then we can make just the right amount.'

'Not a bad idea,' said Cyanide Sid. 'It could be a breakthrough in school catering.'

'Right then, Sid,' said Hairy Harry. 'We'll do a chip count every day just after Assembly, got it?'

Sid agreed that he had got it, and as Assembly was just that minute finishing, he and his leader split up and set off round the school classrooms.

Chapter Five

*

'Right,' said Cyanide Sid, going into Mr Jenkins's classroom where form 4B were preparing to start their day. 'Hands up all those kids who want chips for dinner today.'

All the children, led of course by Billy Baxter in the front row, put up their hands.

'Now then, what is all this?' said Mr Jenkins, putting the register back in his desk and tipping the dinner money he had just finished counting into the tin he always kept it in.

'Well,' said Sid, 'I'm one of the new school cooks, and we've decided to take orders in advance for chips so that we know how many to make – otherwise we make too many or too few. We reckon it's going to be a breakthrough in school catering.'

'I see, well, it sounds like a good idea. I've just finished doing the dinner money actually, so it's most appropriate,' said Mr Jenkins with a friendly smile. 'Come on then, 4B . . . how many chips will each of you want for lunch today?'

Here is the result of the first numerical chip order in the history of world education.

27

NAME	NUMBER OF CHIPS REQUIRED
Brian Fottleton	30
Anne Smith	18
Billy Baxter	180!
Gopal Bannergee	27
Belinda Bollard	14
Yashpal Singh	24
Christopher Tallis	50
Sharon White	3
Jim Tucket	33
Sandra Jarrett	20
James Russell	15
Jane Grant	7
Wes Richards	'Millions'

'That will do, Wes!' said Mr Jenkins. 'You can have twenty-five, I'm sure that's quite enough.'

Sid crossed out 'millions' and put twenty-five in its place. Then he added up the numbers. He made it 446.

'Thank you, form 4B,' he said, and leaving the room he headed off in the direction of the infants' class.

Down the corridor the second years went through the same process with Hairy Harry. Miss Patel finished doing the swimming money and the bookshop stamp money, and then she called the class names out while Harry wrote down the numbers. Then he added them up. It took him quite a long time.

'I make that 490. Thank you very much, kids,' said Harry, and he left the room and went down the corridor to the class next door.

When the two crooked cooks got back into the kitchen, they added up their totals and found that they would have to cook exactly 3,461 chips.

'Incidentally, Boss . . .' said Cyanide Sid, as they

waited for Mrs Gunge to bring in a couple of sacks of potatoes, 'were all the teachers in the classes you went into adding up money?'

'Yes, Sid,' said Hairy Harry, 'they were.'

'So were mine,' said Sid. 'It seems an odd thing for teachers to be doing all the time – I thought they were supposed to *teach* people!'

'Yes, it is pretty odd when you think about it ...' said Harry slowly. 'The kids seem to come to school every day with their pockets full of cash, and then during the morning they hand it all over to the teachers. I reckon there's something *funny* going on!'

'Me too,' said Sid. 'The teachers seem to spend all their time counting money, putting it in tins, and getting children to take it to the office. It's a bit *fishy* if you ask me.'

'I reckon you're right!' said Harry. 'That Head fellow must be making millions. All the money goes down to his office every day. I tell you what – if he doesn't call us in pretty soon, and invite us to share in some of his profits or do a beefy job with him, we may have to get a bit tough with him.' Hairy Harry fondled the sharp edge of his axe with his thumb.

'That's what I like to hear!' said Sid. Although he enjoyed the kitchen work, he was longing to get on with a bit of constructive poisoning.

Chapter Six

In which porridge gets discussed,
and Mrs Gunge gives people ideas.

*

'Well, Mrs Perkins,' said Mr Mackintosh, striding into his office the next day, 'I must say I'm extremely pleased with these new fellows in the kitchens. They're doing a grand job. Would you go and ask them to come up to my office so that I can thank them and discuss a few matters with them?'

Mrs Perkins was not so sure about the new cooks, but she did as she was directed, and moments later Hairy Harry and Cyanide Sid were standing in front of the Head Teacher.

Harry had his hatchet under his kitchen overalls as usual, just in case it would come in handy.

'Now then, it has come to my notice,' said the Head, 'that you two lads are making quite a success of your new job. I really like the way you are taking these chip orders from the pupils – very thoughtful and imaginative of you. However, I think the time has come for me to ask you if you would be willing to move on to something a bit more out of the ordinary – something where you could use the special skills you so obviously have.'

Hairy Harry and Cyanide Sid pricked up their ears. Was the Head going to give them a chance to share in some of his money-making?

31

'I think that chips are all very well,' he continued, 'but children should be given a slightly more varied diet, like I had when I was a young boy in bonny Scotland. Would you mind doing a bit of porridge?'

The effect of this request on two of the most wanted, notorious and noxious criminals in the world today was dramatic. While Mr Mackintosh went on about how good porridge is for the body and soul, Cyanide Sid whispered urgently to Hairy Harry: 'Hey, Harry – "porridge" means a spell in prison, doesn't it? Who *does* he think we are!'

'You're right, Sid,' said Hairy Harry out of the corner of his mouth. 'Look, Mister,' he snarled at the Head Teacher, 'you must think we're nutty. We haven't come here to get landed with doing more porridge. Huh! PORRIDGE! I've done porridge for years and years. The last thing I want at my time of life is to do more blooming porridge!'

'If we'd known this job of yours meant doing porridge, we wouldn't have applied for it,' said Sid indignantly. 'The very thought of having to do more porridge keeps people like me and Harry awake at night.'

Mr Mackintosh was amazed at the new cooks' emotional and passionate response to his simple request.

Harry and Sid marched back to the kitchens. They were very angry.

'What did he go and call us into his office for?' said Sid. 'He doesn't seem to have a job for us at all.'

'Well, I reckon this Head fellow is up to something, and he doesn't want us in on it,' said Harry, gritting his black and misshapen teeth. 'He's collecting all this cash off the kids and we don't seem to be in on

any deals unless we are prepared to go to prison yet again.'

Just then Mrs Gunge shuffled into the kitchen. She had a filthy apron round her shapeless front and a cigarette stuck in her toothless mouth. 'You two thickies should stick up for yourselves a bit more,' she said tauntingly. 'Mackintosh and that Mrs Perkins woman will run rings round you if you don't. They make me sick!'

'We reckon he's up to something,' said Harry slowly, wiping his hairy palms together. 'We reckon he must be the leader of some sort of gang that takes money off kids.'

'Well, I know what I'd do if I was a man,' said Mrs
Gunge.

'What?' asked Sid, with interest.

'I'd bash him on the nut with something heavy and
kidnap him. If he's the leader of a gang, they'd soon
pay a good ransom to get him back.'

The mouths of two of the world's toughest and most expert criminals opened in surprise and amazement at the very idea of it. They both agreed that it was an excellent suggestion.

Chapter Seven

*Which contains the story of some very
remarkable soup.*

*

That night, in his slimy hide-out under the cellar
beneath the waste land, Harry the Hatchet Man
scratched his hairy chin, twiddled his hairy thumbs,
and thought deep thoughts.

'If only . . .' he said suddenly, out loud. 'If only we
had a bit more help . . .'

'What do you mean, Boss?' asked Cyanide Sid.

'Well, if we're going to follow Mrs Gunge's advice,
and start kidnapping a Head Teacher who may very
well be the leader of a gang himself, I reckon we need
more than just the two of us. If *only* I knew where a
few of my old pals were! We need people like Cracker
Crawford the explosives expert, Hans Zupp the Hold-
Up Man, and Nigel Nicker on a job like this!'

'Well, we haven't got them, Boss, so we'll just have to
do the job on our own,' said Sid. 'I think for a start we
will have to refine Mrs Gunge's suggestion – only an
absolute amateur would go and bash someone on the nut
with something heavy in order to kidnap them!'

'What do you mean?' asked Harry, who took a pride
in the way he could bash people on the nut with
something heavy.

'Well, I have special skills with poisons that will do
the job much more effectively. I suggest you leave all

that side of it to me. I'll just pop down to the chemist in the high street for a few rather special supplies; with luck it'll still be open.'

Cyanide Sid put on his coat and stepped out into the late night air. It was cold and very dark. Sid hunched his shoulders and dug his hands deep into his coat pockets. He went across the waste land, through some allotments and down a couple of alleyways near a railway line to reach the car-park at the back of the chemist's.

The lights were still on in the chemist's shop, and through the window he could see a man in a white coat working behind the counter. Good, thought Cyanide Sid, I'm not too late.

He went into the shop and pulled a long shopping list from his coat. He had a lengthy and involved discussion with the man in the white coat, and it took some time for the chemist to make up all the things that Sid wanted.

When Cyanide Sid eventually left the shop, he had a big carrier bag full of bottles and pills and powders in one hand, and his wallet in the other.

Outside he paused for a moment in the darkened doorway of a butcher's shop to push his wallet deep into the inside pocket of his coat. He had just finished doing this when he felt something jab him in the back, and he heard the dreaded words: '*HANSZUPP! Give me that wallet or I'll blow you sky high!*'

Sid swung round. 'Hallo, Hans,' he said with a big smile. 'It's me! Sid!'

'Hallo, Cyanide,' said his attacker. 'Sorry if I gave you a bit of a fright!'

'That's all right, Hans old boy – think nothing of it. Me and the Boss were talking about you only this evening.'

'Really? Well I never,' said Hans Zupp, for, as you will have guessed, this was none other than Hans Zupp, the notorious Hold-Up Man.

'Yes,' continued Sid. 'We're on a job together, and as a matter of fact we could well do with a bit of extra help. Harry was wishing that you and a few of the others were around. Are you busy right now?'

'Not really, in fact I'm pretty bored. I was hoping for a really beefy job to come my way.'

'Splendid! Come back with me now to our hide-out, and we'll explain what we are up to. The Boss will be really pleased to see you!'

So Hans Zupp the Hold-Up Man walked with Cyanide Sid back across the allotments and down to the cellar and, as Sid had predicted, Hairy Harry was extremely pleased to see his old mate Hans again.

Harry and Sid began the next day at school as usual. After Assembly they went round all the classrooms and took the orders for chips. They added all the lists together and worked out that they would need 3,769. Hans Zupp helped Harry with the peeling and chipping of the potatoes while, in a far corner of the kitchen, fat little Cyanide Sid worked intently, all on his own!

He was surrounded by a mass of very mysterious-looking bottles with no labels on them, though he knew what was in each of them. He concentrated on just one school dinner, and by the end of the morning he was extremely pleased with his handiwork.

When the dinner bell went, Billy Baxter and Anne Smith and Belinda Bollard and Jim Tucket and Yashpal Singh and all the other children in the school sat down and started to eat their lunch.

'Look,' said Billy to his friend Jim. 'The cook has made something special for Big Mac.'

This was true. Sid had come out of the school kitchen

with a large bowl of soup, which he'd put down in front of the Head Teacher. 'Here you are, Head Teacher, Sir,' he said. 'I know you like Scottish things, so I've made you a very special soup! It's a broth. I hope you like it.'

'Thank you very much,' said Mr Mackintosh, delighted. 'What's in it?'

'Oh, lots of things!' replied Cyanide Sid.

The Head Teacher and all the children ate their dinner, and while the youngsters went back to their classrooms, Mr Mackintosh, who had enjoyed his soup, went into his office.

In the kitchen the crooks were doing the washing up. Hairy Harry looked even more hideous than usual. He stood at the sink wearing one of Mrs Gunge's flowery aprons, with his great muscly arms in the murky water. His bristly beard stuck out from his cauliflower face: he looked like a gorilla looking through a lavatory brush.

'When will that soup start working?' he asked Sid.

'It will take effect at exactly 2.15. It contains a secret delayed chemical action that I've only just developed – but I am sure it will work. If we ask the Head to come and look at something in the kitchen at 2.15 that should do the trick!'

At just after ten minutes past two, Hairy Harry went to the Head Teacher's office: 'Mr Mackintosh, Sir,' he said urgently, 'we have a crisis in the kitchen. We want you to come and see. We think there is a rat in the fridge!'

'Right. I'll come straight away. The things a Head Teacher has to deal with . . .' said Mr Mackintosh as he strode down the corridor to the kitchen, with Harry following behind him.

'OK!' he said as he entered the room. 'Where's this rat or whatever it is?'

Cyanide Sid glanced anxiously at the clock on the kitchen wall. It said a quarter past two exactly.

Suddenly the Head Teacher stopped speaking. His mouth shut with a snap and his eyes opened wide as if he'd seen a ghost. Then his eyeballs started to rotate, and puffs of green steam came in smoke rings from his ears. His hair stood on end and he started to spin round like a demented ballet dancer.

A split second later his knees collapsed and he was lying senseless on the school kitchen floor, and a minute after that he was trussed up in the back of the getaway van, which Hans Zupp was driving towards the shabby end of the town.

Chapter Eight

In which Mr Jenkins has to take over.

*

Next morning Hairy Harry and Cyanide Sid turned up bright and early for work. So did most of the children, but by the time that they were ready for Assembly, there was no sign of their Head Teacher.

This was because poor Mr Mackintosh was at that moment in the crook's slimy cellar, tied up with his hands behind his back and a blindfold round his eyes, with Hans Zupp the Hold-Up Man keeping watch on him.

When Mrs Perkins opened the post that morning, there was a letter addressed to her that said:

WE HAVE GOT YOUR HEAD TEACHER AND IF YOU DON'T START RAISING SOME MONEY FOR HIM WE WILL START TAKING HIM TO PEECES AND POST-ING THEM TO YOU! SO COFF UP AND LEAVE YOUR DONASHONS ROUND THE BACK OF THE BIKE SHEDS.

ONE WORD TO THE COPS AND WE'LL DUFF YOU UP.

Mrs Perkins read the letter and went straight to the staff room.

'Listen a moment everyone!' she said. 'It would appear from this frightful letter I've just received that our Head Teacher has been kidnapped by a gang of

illiterate ruffians. They are demanding an unspecified ransom, which we have to leave behind the bike sheds. They say that if we inform the police they will duff us up,' she added in a matter of fact tone.

'I rather think that *I* should take charge of this delicate situation,' said Mr Jenkins. 'After all, I am the official Deputy Head.'

The teachers and Mrs Perkins agreed that this was correct.

'I suggest,' said the Deputy, 'that we have a collection. We'll tell the children what has happened and appeal to their generous natures, and those of their parents, and ask them to bring as much money as they can possibly afford to school tomorrow.'

And so it was that Mr Jenkins announced in Assembly that morning a scheme to rescue their beloved Head Teacher.

The children organized collection points in every classroom, and when they went home at the end of the day they had firm instructions to raise as much money as they could for the noble cause. They were to do sponsored spells and swims and reads and runs and walks, and were to get as much cash as possible from their parents.

When Billy Baxter got home that evening he started to tell his mother all about it: 'Can I have some money to take to school tomorrow, Mum?' he said.

'What for now, Billy? I'm always giving you money to take to school! Dinner money, outing money, bookshop money, camp money, swimming money. There's always something!'

'But it's for our Head Teacher, Mum – he's been kidnapped and we are trying to raise some ransom money before the villains who have got him do him any harm.'

45

'Oh well, I suppose it's all in a good cause,' grumbled Mrs Baxter, getting her purse out of her handbag.

In Assembly the next morning, with all the children standing anxiously in rows in front of him, Mr Jenkins, the Deputy Head of St Gertrude's Junior School, made the following announcement:

'Well, now. I am pleased to be able to announce the result of the Save Mr Mackintosh Fund. Mrs Perkins has kindly counted up all the money and has written the amount on this piece of paper for me.'

He took a moment or two to unfold the paper; the whole school tensed in excitement.

'Here then is the result,' he said proudly. 'One pound forty-three pence.'

Chapter Nine

*In which some of the worst crooks in the world
are very disappointed.*

*

'ONE MEASLY POUND FORTY-THREE
PENCE!' exclaimed Cyanide Sid as Hairy Harry the
Hatchet Man opened the envelope that he'd picked up
from the bike sheds that afternoon.

'One pound forty-three pee!' exclaimed Hans Zupp.

'One quid an' forty-three pee,' confirmed Hairy
Harry, counting through the tiny coins in the gigantic
palm of his hand. 'That's all there is, lads!'

The villains felt very disappointed. They had been
looking forward to a really big sum of money. Harry
had even discussed the possibility of putting it in a
bank. He'd never put money in a bank, though he had
taken some out on several occasions.

'This Head fellow of yours can't be leader of much of a
gang if they only go and raise a piffling one forty-three
for him!' said Hans Zupp, feeling really miserable. He
realized that he wasn't on a beefy job after all.

'Well, there's *something* going on at that there
school. I know there is,' said Harry slowly. 'All that
cash flowing around all the time. Where does it all go?
And where does it come from? That's what I'd like to
know! Still, one thing's for certain, we won't get rich
hanging on to this Head Teacher geezer. I'll go and
dump him down on the tip – someone's sure to find him

there in the morning. While I'm gone, you two try to work out what we should do next.'

Hairy Harry the Hatchet Man went to the back of the cellar and picked up the poor Head Teacher. He checked that the blindfold was firmly in place and then, being careful not to make a sound in case his rough voice was recognized, he lifted Mr Mackintosh into an old wheelbarrow and trundled him off to the council rubbish tip at the end of the lane. He deposited the Head and the barrow on top of a pile of old prams and pieces of discarded carpet, and started for home.

Harry was worried about the failure of his kidnap plan, and he walked back towards the lane deep in thought – or as deep in thought as it was possible for him to be. He didn't notice, therefore, two shadowy figures who were standing by some huts at the entrance to the tip.

Harry's hairy head was bent forward on his chest, and his hairy hands were deep in his trouser pockets as he passed the two figures. When one of them stuck out their foot and tripped him up, Harry the Hatchet Man crashed to the ground like a brick kiln chimney that's had dynamite put under it.

'WHAT THE 'ECK'S GOING ON!' he shouted.

'Sorry, mate!' said one of the shadowy figures. 'Are you all right?'

Then both of them bent down and helped the mighty gang leader to his feet. 'Come on, mate, we'll help you up,' they said.

Hairy Harry the Hatchet Man was suspicious – he was sure that they had deliberately tripped him up. When Hairy Harry was suspicious about anything he always did the same thing: he reached for his axe.

'WHAT'S YOUR LITTLE GAME?' he said, and put his hand inside his coat to bring out the mighty hatchet.

It wasn't there.

'Oi!' said Harry with a vicious snarl. 'I've been pick-pocketed! 'Oose nicked my 'atchet!'

Then he noticed that both men were laughing: they were definitely chuckling at him!

'Who *do* you two think you are?' asked Harry in an even more vicious tone, his fists clenching as he spoke.

The reply he got surprised him, and spread a great grin across his hideous face.

'Well, I'm Nigel Nicker, Boss, and this is your old pal, Cracker Crawford!' said the man standing nearest to him.

You need to know a bit about Nigel Nicker. Nigel Nicker was without doubt one of the most accomplished burglars the world has ever known. He was a pickpocket, cat burglar, dog burglar, handbag, wallet, car, van and lorry burglar all rolled into one. He would slink about all night, stealing up drainpipes that didn't belong to him, steal things, and steal back down again. He was an absolute menace. Ugh! A slinky slimy lousy louty menace.

He had absolutely no idea what was his and what was other people's: he'd pinch the milk out of your tea if you weren't careful.

As you will have guessed, Nigel and Harry were old friends and had often worked together in the past.

They shook hands cheerfully and Nigel gave back the axe that he had skilfully removed from the inside of Harry's coat when he had helped him to his feet.

'Good to see you again, Boss,' said Cracker Crawford, lighting a fat cigar. 'We were looking for you actually.

50

In fact, we were whiling the time away with a bit of pocket picking until we found you. Got any work for us?'

'Well now, lads, it just so happens that I might have! Sid and Hans and me have all got a bit stuck with a job we're on, and some help might be just what we need. Follow me!'

And Harry led his two old friends back to his horrible hide-out.

When they got there, Cyanide Sid made a nice pot of tea with some whisky in it, and Harry described the frustrations they were experiencing at St Gertrude's Junior School.

When he had finished, the five criminals had a long discussion. In fact, they plotted and schemed and worked all night through, and by daybreak, as the innocent little birds broke into song for the start of a new dawn, they had come up with a ghastly and original plan.

If it worked it would put them into the *Guinness Book of Records* under 'Most Inventive Mass-Kidnap'.

Chapter Ten

*In which a very unusual school dinner
has a lot of impact.*

*

When the getaway van swept through the gates of St
Gertrude's the next morning, it was heavily laden with
all manner of dangerous things.

Cracker Crawford was responsible for many of them.
Cracker Crawford's main hobby was opening safes. He
did this by putting things into their locks and under
their hinges, lighting the blue touch-paper and standing well back. Safes were not safe from him, and he
was a vital member of Hairy Harry's gang because he
always made things go with a bang.

He was sitting in the back of the van surrounded by
detonators, barbed wire and boxes and boxes of fireworks. There were several bottles and jars that Cyanide Sid had collected together. There was also thirty
pounds of sausage meat and a haggis.

After Assembly a ripple of excitement went round
the whole school, because when the cooks came into
the classrooms to take the orders for chips they made
special announcements.

For instance, when Hairy Harry went into Mr
Harrison's class he gave the following rousing little
speech: 'Right, you kids! We've got a special treat for
you little'uns today. We are going to give you your
very favourite school dinner: *sausage, chips and*

baked beans! Now, come on then – how many chips each?'

Every child's hand shot up. It was their favourite food all right.

When Harry and Sid had been round all the classrooms, Harry went on a special mission to see Mr Mackintosh in his office.

Mr Mackintosh was in a rather shaken state. He had spent most of the previous evening on a dark rubbish tip, doing his best to get free of a rope and a blindfold. In the end he had managed to untie himself and get out from under an old wheelbarrow, and he had got home just before it had started to get light. Like a good Head Teacher he had turned up for school, even though he really needed a day or two off to recover from his recent ordeal.

Hairy Harry knocked on the office door.

'Yes, can I help you?' said Mrs Perkins crisply.

'Err ... I need to see the Head Teacher, please,' replied Harry.

Mrs Perkins did not like the two new cooks at all. She thought that taking orders for chips was disruptive and inefficient. She also knew that there was something very sinister about the men. They were not her idea of nice school cooks, and this one – Hairy Harry – was particularly unpleasant.

'Well, I think he's free,' she said reluctantly, and Harry went in.

'Good morning,' said Mr Mackintosh rather quietly. His head was aching, and his bones felt stiff after the terrible experience of being kidnapped, tied up and blindfolded by persons unknown.

'Good morning, Guv,' said Harry brightly. 'Me and Sid were sorry you had the unpleasant experience of being kidnapped, and we're very pleased that you are

53

back at school now. So we would like to give you and the children a special treat this lunch time. We are doing them sausage and chips, and we thought that you would like something very Scottish. We've got you a haggis!'

'Well, that's very good of you . . .'

'Not at all, Guv, we hope you enjoy it!'

'I'm looking forward to it already,' said Mr Mackintosh, and a happy smile lit up his tired Head Teacher face.

All morning, back in the kitchen, the five crooks were *very* busy. They weren't just making chips: they were making one of the most extraordinary meals ever served for lunch in any school, anywhere. They were pushing forward the frontiers of school cooking.

I only hope your school cooks never do the same.

All the children were eagerly awaiting the dinner bell, and when it rang there was a rush for the dining-hall door. Billy Baxter got there first, but he was closely followed by Jim Tucket, Anne Smith, Belinda Bollard, Sandra Jarrett, Yashpal, Emily and Wes.

Soon they were all sitting down. Mrs Gunge waddled in on her cabbage-stalk legs and went round the tables dishing out the sausage, chips and beans, her mouth blowing in and out like bellows with the exertion. 'Bloomin' blinkin' kids . . .' she muttered as she went, 'should be put down at birth!'

Mr Mackintosh sat at the head of one of the tables, his napkin tucked into his collar and his stomach rumbling at the thought of a delicious haggis.

Everyone was looking forward to a belly-button-rubbing-good meal!

Because it was a special occasion, the Head Teacher said a special St Gertrude's grace: 'For what we are about to receive, may Mrs Gunge be forgiven.'

54

The next moment one hundred children, a Head
Teacher and three members of his staff lifted up their
knives and forks and plunged them into the most
spectacular school dinner in history.

As the metal forks pierced the skin of each sausage,
they triggered off tiny electro-magnetic detonators
that in turn exploded small, individual, stun grenade
stink-bombs buried in the sausages!

The effect was EXPLOSIVE! It was a massive, mega-pong bombshell! The dining hall filled with smoke and horrible fumes, several of the windows blew out, the children and teachers fell choking on to the floor and into their dinners. They grabbed their noses, and their eyes rolled in their sockets at the ghastly whiff!

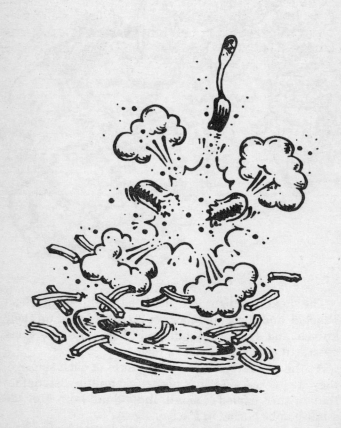

It was all too much for Mr Mackintosh. He tipped over backwards in his chair, his ginger moustache turning up at the ends, and haggis and mashed parsnip spread all over his face.

Several children slumped forwards into their lunches: it was a scene of utter and total wreckage — worse than your bedroom.

Apart from Mrs Gunge and the crooks in the kitchen, only one person in the whole school was not knocked senseless by the terrible smell of banger-and-chip, mega stink-bomb lunches: Mrs Perkins. She had been sitting happily at her desk unpacking her packed lunch when the explosion occurred.

Chapter Eleven

In which a heroine begins to emerge:
and we'll need one!

*

When about a hundred individual sausage stink-bomb stun grenades went off in a room just down the corridor from her, Mrs Perkins knew exactly what to do: she got up and ran as fast as her legs would carry her.

Her bungalow, School View, was just opposite the school gates. Within seconds she was through her front door and on the telephone to Chief Inspector Bollard.

'Hallo, Chief Inspector,' she panted. 'This is an emergency – there has been a terrible explosion at the school, in the dining hall; it was some kind of mega-pong stink-bomb. Bring your men and the fire brigade immediately.'

'Now then . . .' said the Chief Inspector slowly, 'our Belinda was telling me something the other night about the Head Teacher getting kidnapped. It all sounds very fishy to me. I wouldn't be at all surprised if someone wasn't committing an offence up at that there school of yours. But don't worry – we'll be there right away.'

Mrs Perkins put the phone down. She glanced back over the road at the school. Wisps of grey smoke were wafting through the windows, and the building seemed still and eerie.

What she could *not* see was that Hairy Harry the

Hatchet Man and his gang were busy restoring order to the battle-torn school dining hall.

Nigel Nicker and Cyanide Sid were going round the tables, picking up the choking, stinking children and propping them up in what was left of their chairs. Even though they were completely stunned, several of the kids tried to eat the smouldering remains of their sausage-and-chip dinners.

'My word, those bangers were rather good, Sid,' said Nigel Nicker, as he wiped a plateful of beans off the upturned face of Billy Baxter and helped himself to the football stickers from the inside pocket of his blazer. Then he scraped some of the haggis off Mr Mackintosh's chin, pinched his watch, and pushed him and his chair upright again.

Cracker Crawford was also busy. Helped by Hans Zupp, he was rushing round the playground and school building with boxes of fireworks under one arm and plungers and spools of wire under the other. He hadn't been so happy since the last time he was released from prison.

He put huge numbers of rockets, Catherine wheels, Roman candles, Silver Cascades, Fiery Fizzbombs and bangers in the flower beds, beside the bike sheds and under the teachers' cars. He knew all about the use of explosives and their value in fortification. He knew, for instance, that in any building it is the main gate, drive and doorway that are most likely to come under attack, and he acted accordingly.

He also knew that riot police or SAS commandos could attack the school by coming up through the sewers, so he wired up the drains and manholes with all sorts of surprises. By the time he had finished, there was a row of detonator plungers along the back wall of the kitchen.

Hairy Harry himself was converting the whole room into a new siege headquarters for his gang. He rigged up a large megaphone at the window, pointing it down the school drive. He also put a chopping block in the middle of the kitchen, and spent a few happy moments sharpening his axe. A huge hairy smile split his rubbery lips and revealed his blackened, broken teeth as he tested the edge of the axe with his hairy thumb.

Mrs Gunge helped him. 'Cor blimey, Harry,' she chuckled, 'that explosion was just what this school needed! I haven't laughed so much since the day my husband died.'

Then there came the sound that crooks dread all their working lives: the wail of a police car's siren. It came from the road leading to the school gates. Hans and

Cracker rushed inside, and Harry and his gang and Mrs Gunge gathered in their new kitchen headquarters.

They stood on chairs and peered through the high windows. There was a police car right enough, and behind it a fire brigade Landrover and at least two fire engines.

Mrs Perkins also heard the siren and saw the blue flashing lights from her front room. She went out and stood on the front lawn and watched. What she saw next sent a shudder of horror up the back of her green woolly cardigan. As the police car and the fire brigade convoy turned right through the school gates and on to the drive, there was an ear-splitting SWOOOOSH! Earth, flowers and slabs of tarmac flew into the air in a great plume, and the afternoon sky filled with the reek and smoke of hundreds of fireworks.

Up in the school kitchen, Cracker Crawford had been at work with a detonator plunger!

The leading car screeched to a halt with blue smoke rising from its back tyres. Mrs Perkins could not believe her eyes. In front of the car – right beneath its front bumper where there had once been a manhole cover – there was now a massive crater.

Five large and important-looking policemen scrambled out of the car. They all had flat hats and wore black leather gloves. Janet Perkins recognized one of them as Chief Inspector Bollard.

She saw the firemen get out from the fire engines behind too, and they joined the policemen. They were just starting to argue about how to cross the ravine in the school drive, when suddenly a voice that Mrs Perkins instantly knew to be Hairy Harry's split the afternoon air. It came through the megaphone from the school kitchen window:

'RIGHT. THIS IS THE BIGGEST KIDNAP

THE WORLD HAS EVER KNOWN. WE HAVE GOT A WHOLE SCHOOLFUL OF KIDS AND ALL THEIR TEACHERS, AND IF YOU LOT COME ANY NEARER I SHALL PERSONALLY START TO DISMANTLE THEM! WE DEMAND A RANSOM BEFORE WE HAND ANY OF THEM BACK. TEN MILLION QUID WOULD DO NICELY, SO START COLLECTING!'

'Ten million pounds!' Mrs Perkins staggered back in amazement.

'Now look here!' shouted back Chief Inspector Bollard as the policemen and firemen gathered round him in a group. 'I have to advise you that you are all under arrest!'

'WHEN I WANT YOUR ADVICE I'LL ASK FOR IT – FUZZFACE!' said the megaphone.

Inspector Bollard went very red and pretended he hadn't heard.

Chapter Twelve

Don't underestimate a school secretary.

*

From that moment, Mrs Perkins knew that the children and teachers of St Gertrude's Junior School were in *extreme* danger.

She returned to the front room of her little bungalow and scowled in the direction of the school. A determined look came into her eyes. Police and firemen were useless in a situation like this. There was only one person who could save the children now, and that was HER!

Her brows knitted as a forceful frown wrinkled her forehead, and her jaw set like the bow of a proud battleship; she rolled her cardigan sleeves up to expose an ample pair of forearms. 'Right, you crooked cooks. *You won't know what's hit you!*' she said with a snarl, and clenching her massive fists she strode off down the hallway to prepare for a one-woman assault on the school.

She went into her little bedroom at the back of the bungalow and opened the wardrobe door. She took a bullet-proof vest from its dry cleaner's bag and slipped it on under a 'BEWARE – SCHOOL SECRETARY' T-shirt and her second-best green cardigan. I don't want to snag my best woolly, she thought to herself. Then she changed into the most sensible shoes she possessed and put on an old corduroy gardening skirt.

She sat down at her dressing-table and put some things into her largest handbag; they included a black balaclava helmet, a huge tube of mascara, a spare pair of specs, a grappling hook and some rope. Then she made herself a nice cup of tea before going to the broom cupboard and bringing out an old map of the school that she kept there. She stuck it on the front of the pantry door and took a box of map pins from the drawer in the kitchen table.

She studied the map long and hard. She made a mental note of where all the doors were, and the skylights, drainpipes, manholes and windows. She stuck the pins into the map to remind her of these strategic points.

An hour or so later Mrs Janet Perkins was sitting in her front hall waiting for night to fall: she was ready to do her duty. While she waited, she gazed over the road at the barricaded school and wondered how all the poor little children were coping with their terrible ordeal.

She would have been relieved to know that inside St Gertrude's the children had nearly all recovered from the effects of the individual sausage-and-chips, stink-bomb stun grenades. They had helped to get the dining hall back into some sort of order, and were sitting round the tables on the chairs that had not been damaged in the confusion, playing games.

The wicked cooks made them a very nice tea of boiled eggs with thin soldiers of bread, and all the children felt excited at the thought of spending a night in the school. Because they didn't really understand what was going on, they all thought it was quite an adventure!

Mr Mackintosh, Mr Jenkins, Miss Patel and Mr Harrison had also recovered, but were all terrified.

Unlike the children, they felt little sense of adventure. They hardly dared to speak in case the children guessed that they were feeling very frightened.

Outside the school grounds, Chief Inspector Bollard had gathered a whole division of policemen. They had been pouring out of the back of black vans all afternoon dressed in full riot gear, including crash helmets and

shields. By the time it was dark they had surrounded the whole school.

'Those silly policemen are going to be my first problem,' said Janet to herself as she gathered up her handbag and opened the front door of the bungalow.

'May School Sec Force be with me!' she proclaimed. And she stepped out into the chilly night and into action.

Chapter Thirteen

In which Mrs Perkins goes into action.

*

Mrs Perkins closed the door quietly behind her, and put her keys in her coat pocket. She walked down her short drive and turned towards the school gates, where Chief Inspector Bollard and some of his most senior officers were standing in a group with their hands behind their backs.

She went straight up to him. 'Good evening, Chief Inspector,' she said pleasantly. Under her arm she had a large roll of paper.

'Ah! Mrs Perkins. Thank you for your telephone call this afternoon, madam. A right old pickle we are in! We tried to get up to the school but the kidnappers blew up the drive with fireworks; we don't know how to proceed next!'

'I may be able to help you. I have here a map of the school: it will show you where all the doors are and things like that.' She unrolled the map and the Chief Inspector and some of his men helped her to spread it out on the bonnet of a nearby police car.

'My word! This is very useful!' said Chief Inspector Bollard. 'Now then – where do you think the criminals will be situated?'

He and the other officers became very involved in the map, and while they were studying it in the light of their torches, Mrs Perkins slipped away into the inky darkness. Moments later she was through the school gates and darting through the rose bushes that lined the drive. She ran as fast as her sensible shoes would carry her.

She melted into the darkness like a midnight shadow, ducking through the climbing frame, dodging round the swings and the infants' see-saw. By the time she had dived for cover into the sand-pit she was very out of breath. She lay there for a minute or two, recovering.

However, no school secretary pauses for long when there's work to be done, and she soon had her handbag open and was preparing for the next part of her plan of attack. She took out the black balaclava and pulled it over her head; then she squeezed the tube of mascara and smeared the black mixture all over her face. Except for her elasticated stockings, smart glasses and corduroy gardening skirt, she soon looked very like a para commando or a member of the SAS.

She stood up, got out of the sand-pit and slipped silently up to the flower beds under the windows at the side of the school kitchen.

'What was that?' said Hairy Harry in the kitchen. 'I thought I saw something!'

'Where?' asked Cracker Crawford. He joined his boss at the window.

'Out there in the garden,' replied Harry.

'It may be the cops!' said Hans Zupp. 'Keep your eyes open!'

'Don't worry, they won't get very far in the grounds without having a few cracking good surprises,' said Cracker with a nasty sneer.

The night was very dark.

'I must retain the element of surprise,' whispered Janet Perkins to herself. 'They'll have all the doors and windows locked and barricaded – but they won't be expecting an attack through the roof!'

She eyed the school buildings through her long-distance spectacles. Over the kitchens there was a low flat roof, and even in the darkness of the moonless night she could see the large skylights in it.

She crawled through the flower bed until she was against the brickwork. Then she stood up and eased her way along the wall of the school building. She took the throwing line out of her bag, and moments later was whirling the vicious grappling hook in a wide circle above her head like a cowboy with a lasso. She let go and with deadly aim it struck the guttering and stuck there.

It was quite difficult for Mrs Perkins to climb up the rope. She tucked the hem of her skirt into her knickers, and grasped the line in both hands and squeezed it between her feet. It took a lot of heaving and straining and stretching of elastic, but eventually she was able to swing one leg up over the plastic guttering, and with a large sigh of relief she rolled exhausted on to the flat roof.

She paused for a moment or two, partly to see if she had been spotted but mainly to get her breath back.

The night was cold and still. In a distant wood an owl hooted an early evening hoot. But Mrs Janet Perkins was not afraid. She gathered up her trusty handbag and stood up, releasing her skirt and dusting grit from her coat as she did so.

'I don't know why I bothered with this coat,' she said to herself. 'It's hot work climbing ropes!'

She put her handbag down again and unbuttoned the coat. I'll pick it up later, she thought and, peering over the edge of the roof, she dropped the coat down into a rose bed.

What happened next nearly gave Janet a heart attack. There was a horrifying WHOOOOSH! and a rocket shot up into the night sky. It snaked to a halt overhead, and burst in a shower of bright blue stars! The school, its playground and fields and all the surrounding houses were suddenly plainly visible.

Chief Inspector Bollard, who was on watch down by the front gate, had just dropped off to sleep, and he woke with a frightful start: 'Where am I?' he shouted. 'I ARREST YOU!'

'It's another firework, Chief, a rocket,' said Police Constable Jones, who was standing right beside him.

'I wonder what's going on!' added Sergeant Spencer.

Cracker Crawford in the kitchen knew exactly what was going on: 'Oi, Boss! Some snooper's touched one of my rocket flare trip-wires.'

The shock of the trip-wire firework had a disastrous effect on poor Mrs Perkins. Her mouth and eyes opened wide, and she staggered backwards in terror across the flat roof. She didn't stagger for long because she soon came to one of the skylights.

She fell backwards through it and landed in the middle of the school kitchen, right on top of the large chopping block that Hairy Harry the Hatchet Man had put there so carefully earlier that day.

Chapter Fourteen

*In which Chief Inspector Bollard goes
into action, single-handed.*

*

When Mrs Perkins landed on the chopping block in the
middle of the school kitchen, it broke. The noise of
breaking glass, followed by the splintering of timber,
gave Hairy Harry, Cracker Crawford, Cyanide Sid,
Nigel Nicker and Hans Zupp quite a shock.

For a moment or two they didn't know what had hit
them.

Harry was the first to speak: 'SO!' he shouted. 'SO!
A cop disguised as an old woman. We'll have to teach
you a lesson you won't forget, mate!'

'Don't you go calling me "mate",' snapped Janet
Perkins. 'And I'm not a *cop* any more than you are a
cook, you hairy great oaf, I'm a school secretary!' She
got off the broken table and shook bits of glass from
her hair.

'I suggest we tie her up, and sort her out in the
morning,' said Nigel Nicker.

Just then there was a shuffling noise and a smell of
cabbage, and Mrs Gunge came through the door; the
noise had woken her up. 'Well now, what have we got
here?' she said with a sneer. 'Look what Lady Luck
has chucked in through the winder! Mrs High and
Mighty Perkins! Old Bossy Bum!' Mrs Gunge cackled

a hideous laugh. She was delighted to have her old enemy within her grasp.

'She may be a school secretary all right, but I tell yer what, Harry,' said Mrs Gunge, 'I could do with a bit of help in my kitchen. She can start work tomorrow! She can peel all the spuds on her own, and then she can scrub out all the drains. That will soon stop her sounding so blinking bossy and posh!'

Poor Mrs Perkins. Harry snatched her precious handbag from her and Nigel tied her hands behind her back. Then she was thrown like a sack on to some bags of potatoes in the food store. She hardly slept a wink all night.

Though now off-duty, Chief Inspector Bollard didn't sleep very well either. He lay in bed next to the deeply dreaming figure of Mrs Chief Inspector Bollard, in his house at number 999 Letsby Avenue, and he thought . . .

He thought as hard as he could about how to defeat the villains who had kidnapped the entire staff and children of St Gertrude's Junior School – the biggest kidnap plot in the history of crime.

Early in the morning an idea came to him. He sat up in bed, straightened the flat policeman's hat that he always wore, and said, 'I've got it!' Then a bright cheery smile spread across his face. 'Why didn't I think of it before?' he asked himself.

Without waking his wife, he got out of bed and went over to her wardrobe. He took off his dark blue pyjamas and put on one of her party frocks. He added some tights, a headscarf, some high-heeled shoes and her new fur coat. Then he sat down at her dressing-table and busied himself with a lot of make-up.

He drove to the school in his police car and arrived at the gates with a squeal of brakes. 'Right, men!' he said as he got out of the car. 'This will do the trick! Do you know who I am?'

'No, Chief Inspector,' said the policemen round him.

'Good! I shall now proceed into action. I am a master of disguise, and this trick will catch the villains off their guard and enable me to arrest them using surprise and the direct approach. Just watch!'

He pulled the fur coat round his body and started to totter up the school drive, a smile playing on the crooked line of his lipstick.

Hairy Harry, looking through the kitchen window, saw him coming: 'IF YOU COME ANY CLOSER, WE'LL BLOW YOUR BLOCK OFF!' he called through the megaphone.

Chief Inspector Bollard paused and put his hand to his ear as if he couldn't quite hear what had been said. Then he kept on walking.

'Who is it, Boss?' asked Hans Zupp.

'It's a copper dressed up as a woman, and he's pretending he can't hear me! I'll teach him!' said Harry with a deep laugh.

The Chief Inspector got to the front door of the school. What the crooks did not know was that beneath his fur coat he had concealed his extra-long riot police truncheon . . .

'Let's go and see what he wants,' suggested Harry. He led the way to the front door and opened it.

'Ahhh . . . good morning, my good men,' said Chief Inspector Bollard in a high, faltering, reedy voice. 'I wonder if you can help me . . . I'm only a poor defenceless woman . . . my little nephew comes to this school and I have just arrived to see him . . . will you please let me inside?' He gave the crooks a crooked lipstick smile.

'NO!' said Hairy Harry.

'Why ever not, my good man?' asked the Chief Inspector in his wavering auntie voice.

'BECAUSE YOU AIN'T NOBODY'S AUNTIE!' bellowed the villains' boss.

'Oh yes I am!'

'Well, why have you got a black moustache, and a cop's flat hat under your headscarf then? TWIT!' said Hairy Harry.

Before Chief Inspector Bollard could think of a sensible answer to this sensible question, Harry hit him over the head with a sockful of flour that he had kept hidden behind his back for that very purpose.

The master of disguise sank lifeless on to the front step of St Gertrude's Junior School.

'Bring him in, lads,' said Harry. 'WE'LL DEAL WITH HIM LATER!'

Chapter Fifteen

Which deals with Mrs Gunge.

*

Once Chief Inspector Bollard had been dragged in through the front door and been shut in the school book cupboard, Hairy Harry decided that it would be a good idea to start off the first full day of the kidnap with an Assembly.

He and his gang strode into the dining hall where all the staff and children were finishing their breakfast.

'Right!' he said, standing at the front of the hall and addressing them in his deep rough voice. 'Me and my staff here' – he waved a hand in the direction of his gang who were lined up behind him – 'have decided that we might as well let the teachers go. After all, they seem to fetch very little: we only got one pound forty-three for the Head Teacher!'

There was a gasp from everyone in the room, especially Mr Mackintosh. They hadn't realized that Hairy Harry and his gang had been his kidnappers.

'We reckon,' went on Harry, 'that you kids, as a job lot, are worth at least ten million quid, and we're demanding the money from your parents and grannies and people like that. They'll pay up because they'll want you back safe and sound: they're funny like that!'

'Hey, Billy,' said Yashpal to Billy Baxter in a whisper,

'you may have been good at getting us chips to eat, but I'd like to see you get us out of this mess!'

'You never know, there may be a way,' said Billy out of the corner of his mouth.

'Assembly over,' announced Hairy Harry. Then he beckoned Mr Mackintosh and the other teachers to the front, and Cyanide Sid and Nigel Nicker pushed them into freedom through the front door.

In the school kitchen, meanwhile, Janet Perkins was having a hard time.

She had heard Hairy Harry shouting through the megaphone when Chief Inspector Bollard had come up the drive in disguise, and she had heard the kerfuffle at the front door. She had even heard the noise of the unconscious police chief being locked in the school book cupboard, but she had not paid much attention. She had been too busy peeling potatoes.

Although she was a school secretary with nerves of steel, she knew that in her present circumstances resistance was useless. For the time being she had to bear the taunts of the terrible Mrs Gunge, and she had to get on with the tasks that the crooked cooks set her. So she peeled and scraped and mopped and scrubbed and rubbed and polished and skivvied and slaved.

But while she worked she also watched and waited. She was ready to take advantage of any opportunity that might present itself. James Bond or Indiana Jones would have done the same.

Her chance came just before lunch.

She had been locked in the food store all day, because Hairy Harry and his men didn't like having her in the kitchen, which was their headquarters. She was rolling out some pastry with a rolling pin.

Mrs Gunge came in to get something. 'Huh!' she said with a horrible sneer. 'That idiot Harry has let the

78

teachers go! He could at least have chopped a few of them up first. If I'd been him I would have taught that Head Teacher a lesson with my axe. Head*less* Teacher would have been a bit more like it! With a bit of luck he'll start mincing up some of the kids soon.'

As Mrs Gunge finished this frightful speech, Mrs Perkins went into action with the speed of a rattle-snake. She bopped Mrs Gunge a very sharp blow on the top of the head with her rolling pin. A second later

Mrs Gunge lay like a pile of dirty washing on the concrete floor. Mrs Perkins removed Mrs Gunge's dirty old flowered dress, her greasy apron, her crumpled, rumpled stockings, her smelly old shoes and the duster that she wore on her head.

Unlike Chief Inspector Bollard, Mrs Perkins *was* a master of disguise. She put Mrs Gunge's filthy clothes on. It was very brave of her to do it, but she regarded it as her duty as a caring school secretary.

She spread some white lard over her face to give it Mrs Gunge's greasy complexion. Then she took some bristles from her pastry brush and pushed them into

lumps of lard that she stuck on her chin, and then she stuffed rashers of bacon down inside the stockings to make her legs look more like Gunge legs – all lumps and bumps and veins. Ugh! She put bits of bread and bags of flour into the dress to make it more shapeless and saggy, and she practised shuffling and blowing through her gums like Mrs Gunge did.

Mrs Gunge, meanwhile, was lying on the floor in her underwear. It was not a pretty sight: I advise you to turn your head away when you read this next bit. She had long khaki knickers that came down to her white knees and a sort of corset and suspender thing that seemed to be made out of grey canvas. Lying there, she looked like an old scout tent that had collapsed in a storm.

When Janet felt that her disguise was complete she waddled out of the food store. She went straight past Hairy Harry and Cracker Crawford who were on duty in the kitchen, and out into the school dining hall.

The crooks and children ignored her: the trick was working!

Mrs Perkins did her Gunge shuffle across the room. Though she worked hard to get the walk right, and the puffing through the gums, she kept her eyes sharply on the children. She was looking for Billy Baxter. At last she spotted him on the far side of the room.

She shuffled over and bent down behind his chair, pretending that she was picking something up off the floor. 'Billy ... Billy Baxter,' she said in a hissed whisper. 'It's me, Mrs Perkins – not Mrs Gunge. I'm in disguise. Listen carefully ...'

Billy could hardly believe it.

'I have infiltrated the gang of villains. Tell all the children to be ready for anything! Watch out for any

81

signals I may give you, and use your initiative. We've got to retain the element of surprise.'

'OK,' whispered Billy.

'We'll need to pick them off one by one. Good luck,' added Mrs Perkins.

Billy could hardly believe his ears: he'd always thought of Mrs Perkins as an ordinary school secretary – firm on the surface but kind and helpful underneath. Here she was, sounding like a hero from a TV thriller!

Billy got to work whispering to all the children the remarkable news of Mrs Perkins's conversation with him, and he impressed on them the importance of being watchful, alert and ready for anything!

Chapter Sixteen

In which almost anything could happen.

*

When Mrs Perkins returned to the kitchen in her disguise, she found Cracker Crawford sitting in front of the row of detonators on a box marked 'DANGER FIREWORKS – ASSORTED BANGERS'.

'Good morning, Mrs Gunge,' he said with a cheery smile. He took a puff at his fat cigar.

'Morning, my duck,' replied Mrs Perkins in a Gungey voice. 'How's this here kidnap going then?'

'Oh, not too badly, I suppose. I must say, I could be doing with a bit more activity.' Cracker put his cigar down in an ashtray on a stool beside him. 'Personally, Mrs Gunge,' he said, 'I get a bit bored when there are no cracking good explosions going on. I'm a man of action! I like a whiff of cordite in the air, and a bit of powder and shot!'

He rubbed his chin and thought about this as he said it.

Janet Perkins again went into action with rattlesnake-like speed. She bent down and picked up Cracker Crawford's cigar. The end of it was glowing nicely. She saw that the twisted blue touch-paper of a large Blockbuster Banger was sticking out of the top of the box he was sitting on. She touched it with the glowing tip of the cigar, and nipped outside through the kitchen door.

83

'Yes,' he went on, 'the more I think about it, the more I realize that I am the sort of man who needs to do things, and go places! Sitting around just doesn't suit my personality.'

He reached down for his cigar, but before he could touch it there was the most almighty BANG!

Cracker Crawford went places all right. The spontaneous combustion of a full box of assorted bangers blew him backwards into the air, and when he came down he landed slap-bang on the top of one of his detonator plungers. This caused a second firework display that had interesting results.

As you know, Cracker Crawford had spent quite a lot of the previous afternoon fixing up defences round the school. The fireworks under the school drive had already been effective. The plunger that his senseless body now happened to fall on was the one connected to several huge boxes of Roman candles in the school's sewers.

It was just Hans Zupp's bad luck that he happened to be sitting on the lavatory at the time that the fireworks went off.

BANGGGGG!

Hans went straight up through the fragile asbestos roof of the boys' toilets like a man in an ejector seat.

'OH MY GOOD GAWD!' he shouted. *'The lavatory's on fire!'*

He went up so high that he managed to get the singed remains of his trousers up even before he started to come down again. When he did come down he landed in the infants' sand-pit, not far from the side door to the kitchen and right beside Mrs Perkins.

She knew exactly what to do. She gave him a swift karate chop and he instantly fell into unconsciousness

– a smouldering and lifeless heap, face down in the soft sand.

'Two down: three to go,' said Mrs Perkins, dusting her hands on her pinny.

As she did so, she was watched by Billy Baxter and most of the children from the dining hall. They had seen Hans Zupp's spectacular landing in the sand-pit and what had happened to him at the mighty hands of their school secretary.

Cyanide Sid, guarding the children, had also seen it.

No crook likes to see another member of his gang being assaulted by a school dinner lady, and the moment Sid saw it he flew into action. He rushed to one of the windows, opened it and bellowed: *'I saw that! I'm coming to get you! You're going to come to a very nasty end!'*

You will probably have realized that Cyanide Sid was no simple, bash-them-on-the-bonce sort of baddy. He was much cleverer and more technological. Many people who had got on the wrong side of him in the past had finished their days in poisoned agony. Their last moments had been writhing, scalding and terrible!

Even now he was looking forward to concocting something fiendishly awful for Mrs Perkins. All he needed to do was capture her alive. He was too fat to fit through the window, so he made a charge for the door.

In that split second Billy Baxter saw his chance. Almost without thinking about it, his hands searched inside his blazer pockets and brought out two fistfuls of marbles. He flung them on the floor in front of the podgy little poisoner.

The moment the other children saw what he had done, they too went into action. As Cyanide Sid's feet went from under him, brave Belinda Bollard dived head-first at his fat belly, Yashpal went for his throat, and child after gallant child piled down on top of him as he crashed to the floor in a blubbery heap.

'Oi! Get off!' yelled the startled criminal.

'Shut up, Fatso!' shouted Billy from half-way up the pile of people.

Within minutes the winded and bruised villain was trussed with satchel straps to the leg of a dining-hall table, with a gag in his mouth and his chef's hat pulled down firmly over his piggy little eyes.

The pupils of St Gertrude's were pleased with their handiwork, and so was Mrs Perkins who had watched them through the window.

'Three down,' she said. 'Two to go.'

Chapter Seventeen

*In which we discover that boxes of fireworks
can do a lot of damage.*

*

There were other important results from simultaneous
explosions of a box of assorted bangers in the kitchen
and the blast of hundreds of Roman candles in the
school sewers, apart from the fact that Hans Zupp
went into sub-orbital flight above the boys' toilets.

For instance, the kitchen sinks exploded, and this in
turn blew a large hole in the kitchen wall. Hairy
Harry and Nigel Nicker had been finishing a bit of
washing up when it happened, and the blast threw
them both backwards across the kitchen. Nigel dived
under one of the worktops, and Harry ended up with
his head in one of the ovens.

The policemen down at the school gates saw the wall
of the kitchen blow out, and saw a tall cloud of smoke
and dust rise up into the mid-morning sky. They feared
the worst not just for the schoolchildren, but also for
their own dear Chief Inspector who had disappeared
through the front door of the building earlier that
morning.

They need not have worried too much.

As you know, Hairy Harry the Hatchet Man had
coshed poor Chief Inspector Bollard with a sockful of
flour, and the crooked cooks had dragged him into the
school and shut him in the book cupboard. However,

when the school sewers exploded, the noise and shock had roused him.

At first he had wondered what he was doing in a dark cupboard in a party frock and fur coat, with a headscarf over his policeman's flat hat, but slowly it all came back to him.

A smell of smoke and fireworks also came to him, so he decided that the best thing to do would be to get out of the cupboard before it became his grave. He smashed the door open with his shoulder.

Outside in the main school corridor there was chaos. Although he was still in a dazed state from the blow on the head, he soon realized that the building was full of smoke and that children were shouting and screaming, and water was pouring across the floor from fractured plumbing.

He hadn't been so confused since the police station's last Christmas party.

He stumbled through a door marked 'kitchen' and then, in an attempt to get outside into the fresh air, he staggered through another door. Unfortunately for him, he had gone into the food store.

He fell over what he thought was a sack of potatoes, but which was actually the groaning figure of Mrs Gloria Gunge in her underwear. He fell full length on the floor, but the shock of his arrival must have revived Mrs Gunge because she slowly stood up.

The Chief Inspector picked himself up too, but when he turned round and saw the hideous sight of Mrs Gunge in her semi-naked state, he did the only sensible thing he could in the circumstances. He fainted.

Mrs Gunge did a sensible thing too. Dressed as she was in only her khaki corsetry and suspenders, she was feeling very chilly. She couldn't help noticing that the man who had just barged into the room was wearing an expensive fur coat.

Almost before the Chief Inspector hit the ground, she whipped it off him and put it on. Then, as an extra precaution, she picked up the rolling pin that Mrs Perkins had left on the floor, and gave him a smartish bash on the hat with it.

Chapter Eighteen

In which, unfortunately, Hairy Harry comes round.

*

From the time when the school kitchen sinks had exploded and the kitchen wall blown out, Hairy Harry the Hatchet Man had been lying with his head in one of the school ovens. He had been stunned by the blast.

Hairy Harry's head, however, was made almost entirely of bone, and it would have taken quite a lot to damage it permanently. After a minute or two he awoke from his temporary slumber. He took his head out of the oven, rubbed it, gave it a shake and stood up.

Mrs Gloria Gunge, who was now hiding in the food store dressed in Chief Inspector Bollard's wife's fur coat, decided that she had had quite enough excitement for one day, and that it might now be a good idea if she was to step over the lifeless form of Chief Inspector Bollard and make a run for home. After all, she did now have a lovely new fur coat to hide the fact that she was only in her underclothes.

She opened the store door and stepped out into the kitchen. She saw the brand-new hole in the wall where the sinks had recently been, and she walked through it and out into the midday sun.

She did not see Hairy Harry standing by the oven because of all the smoke and plaster dust; but he saw her. Or rather, he thought he saw someone in a fur coat walking past him through the ruins of his kitchen headquarters. He jumped to the conclusion that it was Chief Inspector Bollard, still disguised in a lady's fur coat and now escaping!

Harry's criminal mind saw the chance to retrieve something from his disastrous situation. If he didn't let the important policeman get away he might be able to ransom him, or use him as a shield from police marksmen while he made a safe getaway.

Harry went into action. He picked up the sockful of flour that he had already used once with such good effect that day, strode through the hole in the wall and sloshed the figure in the fur coat with it.

Mrs Gloria Gunge fell to the ground for the second time since breakfast.

Hairy Harry was just about to lift his prey and drag it back into the kitchen, when his eyes chanced to fall on some activity in the nearby play area.

Mrs Perkins, pleased with the work the children had done on Cyanide Sid in the dining hall, had now turned her attention once more to the smouldering figure of Hans Zupp. She was busily tying his shoe laces together in case the effects of the karate chop wore off.

'OI!' shouted Harry. 'WHAT THE HECK DO YOU THINK YOU'RE DOING?'

Janet looked up and saw him. He looked like a cross between Goliath and a mountain bear with a sockful of flour in its paw. She did what you, or I, or any sensible person would have done: she ran round the back of the school as fast as she possibly could.

Hairy Harry followed her with ground-shuddering strides.

Chapter Nineteen

Now a division of riot police goes into action!

*

You will remember that the sound of the recent explosions, and the tall column of smoke that stood in the sky above the school, had worried the policemen down at the school gates.

'Look, Sarge, what are we going to do?' asked PC Jones anxiously.

'I'm not sure,' said Sergeant Spencer. 'We've already lost our Chief Inspector and the whole place is obviously mined with millions of fireworks. To rush in now could be very dangerous.'

Just as he and some of the other officers were thinking about the problem, they heard a terrible wailing shriek.

'HELP, H E L P!'

The lines of riot police drew back as up the road ran a very distraught lady. Sergeant Spencer, Police Constable Jones and some of the other officers instantly recognized her: it was Anita Bollard – their Chief Inspector's wife.

'IT'S TOO AWFUL!' she wailed, tears running down her cheeks. 'It's *terrible*! I can't believe it! *It's the end of my life!*'

PC Jones and Sergeant Spencer tried to calm her: 'Now don't take on so, Mrs Bollard – he may not be harmed after all. We'll get him back for you. We're trying hard to think of a way to rescue him.'

'What are you two idiots talking about?' yelled Mrs Bollard. 'I'm not fussed about my husband: SOMEONE'S PINCHED MY FUR COAT!'

The Sergeant and all the other policemen looked up the drive towards the school. They all had vivid memories of the last time they had seen the coat, and of the wobbling figure of their commander as he had tottered off in it to almost certain death.

You will understand, therefore, that they were all extremely surprised when they saw, at that moment, a very furtive and ferrety man nipping through the school rose beds in Mrs Bollard's coat!

It was none other than Nigel Nicker.

You will remember that at the time of the massive firework explosion, Nigel had dived under one of the worktops in the school kitchen. After a little while, he had decided that it might be best to come out and attempt to steal away before anyone noticed him. (He was always stealing things.)

He had come out of the kitchen through the hole in the wall, and he had just been stepping over the groaning figure of Mrs Gunge, when he noticed that she was wearing a very expensive fur coat. As you know, Nigel had not pinched anything worthwhile for days and days. Here was a splendid opportunity to salvage something from the disastrous St Gertrude's kidnap!

He soon had Mrs Gunge out of the coat and back in nothing but her terrible underclothes. He popped the fur on, and was making a crafty dash through the gardens when the policemen saw him.

'GET HIM!' yelled Anita Bollard at the top of her

voice, and a whole division of riot police flew into action.

Nigel saw them coming and doubled back towards the rear of the school, hoping to lose them in the smoke and general confusion. He realized afterwards that this was probably a big mistake.

The police ran fast; they hadn't been doing very much recently and they felt that the exercise would do them good. PC Jones led the charge, but as they sped up the drive he was neck and neck with Anita Bollard: the sight of her precious fur coat spurred her into extra effort!

Nigel Nicker was an old hand at running away from cops, and he was generally very good at it. What went wrong this time was that as he shot round the corner on the far side of the school, he ran head-first slap-bang into the large frame of Mrs Janet Perkins.

Chapter Twenty

In which one more goes down,
but there is still one left to go.

*

The sturdy form of Mrs Perkins had been travelling at top speed – mainly because Hairy Harry the Hatchet Man was after her. Nigel Nicker was moving quickly too, in his ferrety, nippy way.

It was rather like a small speedboat hitting a battleship: both boats sank. Nigel Nicker fell to the ground, stunned, winded, and definitely done for. Janet didn't feel too good either. She was not used to being run into by robbers on the run, and she sank in confusion to the ground.

Luckily for her, the collision had taken place beneath the dining-hall window – the window that Cyanide Sid had opened a little earlier in order to shout at her. Billy Baxter and the other children had seen the disastrous collision and its consequences, and knew that they would need to act promptly to assist their distressed school secretary.

'Come on!' said Billy, and led by him the brave children poured as fast as they could through the open window.

While some of them started to tie up the unconscious Nigel Nicker, Belinda and Yashpal fanned Mrs Perkins's face. Billy and Jim Tucket and Wes Richards got behind her and tried to lift her to her feet. They didn't find it easy.

'Watch out, children,' mumbled Mrs Perkins, 'the gang leader is after me. He's very dangerous!'

'Quick!' said Billy urgently. 'Get her into the store!'

With a great deal of straining, they managed to drag the dazed secretary in through a door that led via a short corridor to the food store and kitchens. It was usually used to deliver food to the school. Once inside, the children of 4B did their best to stand Mrs Perkins up and help her regain her composure.

Outside, in the school playground, all the children of St Gertrude's were escaping through the open dining-hall window.

Inside, deep within the food store itself, Chief Inspector Bollard was coming round for the second time that day. His head hurt terribly from the recent bash with the rolling pin. It also hurt terribly from the earlier bash with the sockful of flour. But like all high-ranking policemen, the Chief Inspector was tough. He stood up, dusted down his party frock, straightened his hat and headscarf and picked up the rolling pin.

He hitched up his wife's dress, ran through the doorway to the kitchen, and dashed out through the hole in the wall into the afternoon sunshine. His eyes were just growing accustomed to the bright light when he saw a large figure lumbering towards him. You've guessed it: Hairy Harry the Hatchet Man!

Harry had been right round the school twice looking for Mrs Perkins. The second time round he'd had to hurdle over quite a few escaping infants who were now littering the playground. Luckily for them, he was concentrating on finding Mrs Perkins.

Hairy Harry was not in a good mood. He was pretty dangerous when he was feeling happy; when angry, he was absolutely lethal.

Now, there in front of him, in party frock and police hat, stood the copper he thought he had locked in the book cupboard *and* coshed twice with a sockful of heavy flour!

'RIGHT, FUZZFACE!' he yelled. *'I'm going to chop you up right now!'*

Harry advanced like a gorilla with a headache and drew his wicked hatchet from inside his cook's jacket. Chief Inspector Bollard raised the rolling pin. They

100

began to circle each other in the playground – like boxers at the start of round one.

They were hardly aware of the crowd that was forming in an awestruck circle around them. It consisted of schoolchildren and the riot police who had just rushed up the drive behind PC Jones and Mrs Bollard.

'My hero!' said Anita Bollard, gazing towards her gallant husband.

'. . . And your party dress,' whispered PC Jones beside her.

Chapter Twenty-One

In which Hairy Harry decides to bury the hatchet.

*

The crowd hushed, the birds fell silent and time stood still, as the two adversaries – Hairy Harry the Hatchet Man and Chief Inspector Bollard – wheeled round each other in the school playground. The afternoon sun glinted on the keen steel of Harry's hatchet, and on the sequins of the Chief Inspector's shoulder straps.

Hairy Harry swung once or twice with the hatchet but the Chief Inspector dodged back, avoiding its cruel edge.

'I'm going to chop you into Oxo cubes!' sneered the world's most dangerous criminal.

'You're going to help me with my inquiries!' snarled back the nation's bravest police officer.

Again Harry swung the axe. This time, as Chief Inspector Bollard stepped back to avoid the blow, his left foot slipped into the infants' sand-pit. His high-heel shoe stuck deep into the sand!

He sank down, off-balance, on one knee. Hairy Harry saw his chance and raised the axe two-handed above his head. The crowd held its breath, but before Harry could bring the hatchet down, the Chief Inspector flung the rolling pin straight at Harry's hairy face.

Harry ducked. The rolling pin caught him a glancing blow on the side of the head and spun off over the top of the crowd.

'AHHH! NOW YOU'RE FOR IT, FUZZFACE!' roared Harry, as the Inspector rolled across the sand-pit.

Sergeant Spencer and PC Jones could bear it no longer. Their gallant commander, sweat running in rivulets down his make-up, was now defenceless.

'Come on, Jones!' said the Sergeant. 'I'm going in with my truncheon – you follow with handcuffs and get in there quick!'

The brave Sergeant raised his anti-riot truncheon above his head and rushed towards Hairy Harry, who was lumbering after the Chief Inspector as he made a scuffling retreat on all fours towards the climbing frame.

Sergeant Spencer was nearly up to him when Harry heard him and turned round. With a vicious, hairy-fisted punch he sent the officer reeling backwards into the arms of PC Jones.

'I'LL DEAL WITH YOU TWO TWITS IN A MINUTE!' growled Harry.

Then he turned again on the Chief Inspector, who had now scrambled into the space in the middle of the climbing frame. Harry swung the axe at him time and time again, its sharp edge catching the metal tubing in a shower of sparks.

The valiant Chief Inspector was caught like a rat in a trap.

Harry started clambering in through the frame, but the Chief Inspector rolled out under it and ducked down beneath the swings. Harry followed, brushing the chains and seats aside as if they were dry grasses.

The Chief Inspector ran round the see-saw once or twice but on the second circuit he tripped and fell, spread-eagled beside the see-saw.

By the time that Mrs Perkins had got her breath

103

back in the food store, and had been helped outside through the hole in the kitchen wall by Billy Baxter and his friends, she emerged to see Hairy Harry raise his axe once more above his head, high above the defenceless figure of poor Chief Inspector Bollard!

Chapter Twenty-Two

Which brings our story to a close.

*

Does your school secretary move fast in an emergency?

Mrs Perkins was across that playground before you could say 'dinner lady'. She galloped her way through the struck-dumb riot police like a rhino that's sat on a tintack.

Before anyone else could move she was at the scene of the duel and, like a rugger player scoring the most dramatic try, she dived full pelt at the 'up' end of the see-saw. The end that was down shot skywards with the speed of a rocket, and it caught Hairy Harry crash-bang under his hairy horrible chin!

It lifted him off the ground; black broken teeth flew in all directions, and his axe fell harmlessly to the earth behind him. When his feet touched the ground again, he gave his last and mightiest roar and, like a slain ox, he toppled backwards on to the grass.

Mrs Perkins, accompanied by Billy and most of the children from 4B, came down on him like a ton and a half of lead bricks! A cloud of dust billowed into the air, and in the nearby rookery the birds rose cackling into the afternoon sky.

When they got back on to their feet, Hairy Harry still lay there groaning. He looked like a beached whale with a hangover.

105

'Five down,' said Mrs Perkins straightening her back and dusting herself down. 'None to go.'

Then the police got busy. They picked up poor Sergeant Spencer and revived him and PC Jones; they put handcuffs on Hairy Harry and Hans Zupp and Nigel Nicker; they gave Mrs Bollard her coat back. They went into the school dining room and brought out the trussed-up figure of Cyanide Sid, and they searched the school kitchens and found Cracker Crawford. His eyebrows were missing, and his clothes were smouldering from the after-effects of the assorted bangers, but he was still breathing, so they handcuffed him as well and defused all the remaining detonator plungers.

As the sun began to sink below the top-most branches of the beech trees that lined St Gertrude's football pitch, Chief Inspector Bollard cleared his throat, straightened his headscarf, and walked with limping steps to the foot of the climbing frame that had so nearly been the scene of his last mortal moments. He climbed up a few rungs as the crowd of smiling children assembled in a circle round him.

'BOYS AND GIRLS,' he called out, his manly voice ringing round the playground. *'You and your young leader, Billy Baxter, are to be congratulated on the quick-witted way you behaved today, and I am pleased to announce that the kidnap and siege of St Gertrude's Junior School is now officially over!'* A huge cheer went up from the crowd of children. *'You youngsters can all go home, and the villains are now helping me and my officers with our inquiries. They are not likely to be out and about for quite a long time!'*

Again the children cheered.

'However . . .' went on the Chief Inspector. *'I think you all know the enormous debt of gratitude that we owe to your gallant school secretary, Mrs Perkins!'* There was an earsplitting cheer, and several of the policemen lifted Mrs Perkins on to their shoulders – though afterwards they slightly regretted it because she was rather heavy.

'I myself, as you all witnessed, owe her my life! If it wasn't for her, I would at this moment be looking like a bowl of dog's dinner. Three cheers for Mrs Perkins!'

As the cheering died down, the Chief Inspector's voice rang out once more: *'I intend to recommend Mrs*

Janet Perkins for the highest award for bravery the police force can give: *for gallantry in going to the aid of an officer in distress. Or in THIS DRESS, I should say!'*

The sound of laughter filled the warm dusky air.

Much later that evening, Mrs Perkins put out her cat and poured out her cocoa. She sat on the end of her bed in her little bedroom at the back of the bungalow and took off her bullet-proof vest. She sipped her drink as she wearily eased off her sensible shoes.

'I know one thing,' she said to herself as she did so. 'I need an early night after all that exertion; *there's a lot more to being a school secretary than most people imagine!'*

Some other Puffins

VERA PRATT AND THE BISHOP'S FALSE TEETH

VERA PRATT AND THE FALSE MOUSTACHES

Brough Girling

The hilarious, fast-moving adventures of Wally Pratt and his motorbike-riding, fanatical mechanic of a mother.

SADDLEBOTTOM

Dick King-Smith

Hilarious adventures of a Wessex Saddleback pig whose white saddle is in the wrong place, to the chagrin of his mother.

THE BEAST MASTER

Andre Norton

Spine-chilling science fiction – treachery and revenge! Hosteen Storm is a man with a mission to find and punish Brad Quade, the man who killed his father long ago on Terra, the planet where life no longer exists.

WOOF!

Allan Ahlberg

Eric is a perfectly ordinary boy. Perfectly ordinary, that is, until the night when, safely tucked up in bed, he slowly turns into a dog! Fritz Wegner's drawings superbly illustrate this funny and exciting story.

JELLYBEAN
Tessa Duder

A sensitive modern novel about Geraldine, alias 'Jellybean', who leads a rather solitary life as the only child of a single parent. She's tired of having to fit in with her mother's busy schedule, but a new friend and a performance of 'The Nutcracker Suite' change everything.

THE PRIESTS OF FERRIS
Maurice Gee

Susan Ferris and her cousin Nick return to the world of O which they had saved from the evil Halfmen, only to find that O is now ruled by cruel and ruthless priests. Can they save the inhabitants of O from tyranny? An action-packed and gripping story by the author of prize-winning THE HALFMEN OF O.

THE SEA IS SINGING
Rosalind Kerven

In her seaside Shetland home, Tess is torn between the plight of the whales and loyalty to her father and his job on the oil rig. A haunting and thought-provoking novel.

BACK HOME
Michelle Magorian

A marvellously gripping story of an irrepressible girl's struggle to adjust to a new life. Twelve-year-old Rusty, who had been evacuated to the United States when she was seven, returns to the grey austerity of post-war Britain.